Visit us on the Web!
StepIntoReading.com
randomhousekids.com

Educators and librarians, for a variety of teaching tools, visit us at RHTeachersLibrarians.com

ISBN 978-0-7364-3367-9 (trade) — ISBN 978-0-7364-8200-4 (lib. bdg.) — ISBN 978-0-7364-3368-6 (ebook)

Printed in the United States of America   10 9 8 7 6 5 4 3 2 1

DISNEY · PIXAR

THE GOOD DINOSAUR

CRASH, BOOM, ROAR!

By Susan Amerikaner

Illustrated by the Disney Storybook Art Team

Random House 🏠 New York

Poppa hears a sound.

What is it?

Crack. Crack! CRACK!

It is Arlo!

Arlo hears the river.

Burble. Bubble. Gurgle!

Arlo hears a storm.

Crash. Boom. Bang!

Spot and Arlo howl.

Yoooooowwww!

Arlo and Spot play.

Animals pop up.

Pop. Pop! POP!

A T. rex ROARS!

Spot bites.

Arlo yells.

Owwww!

OUCH!

Arlo hears a fire.

Hiss. Crackle. Snap!

Arlo hears Momma.

ARLO!

Momma hears Arlo.

MOMMA!

The sound of home
is the best sound of all!